Flippy & Dotty

Go to The Pond

Story and Illustrations By Sophie Blokker

Dotty the dog and Flippy the frog,

were the best of friends who loved to just play,

so they went to the pond on a hot summers day.

When they got to the pond, Flippy jumped in,

and started to show how well he could swim.

Dotty sat by the side of the pond, fresh and deep,

afraid to jump in, and started to weep.

Flippy shouted to Dotty

"Come on in, come on in!"

But Dotty replied to his friend

"I can't swim".

"I'll watch you swim," said Dotty

"I'll just sit on this log"

"I'm not going to swim,

I'm a dog not a frog".

As Dotty watched Flippy,

He stopped feeling weepy,

and started to feel, a little sleepy.

As Dotty just rested, he started to dream,

He dreamt he was eating a strawberry ice cream.

His eyes slowly closed...

THEN he slipped off the log...

...With a

SPLOSH!!

On top of his friend Flippy frog!

Dotty woke with a fright! And he gave out a yelp!

His friend Flippy frog said "Don't worry, I'll help"

But Dotty the dog just splish splashed about,

And he paddled so fast he was suddenly out!

"You can swim!!" shouted Flippy

"You can swim like a frog!!"

"NO!" shouted Dotty

"I can swim like a dog!!".

So Flippy and Dotty, decided to stay,

And play in the pond all that hot sunny day.

They jumped and they swam,

And they floated about,

And they played lots of games,

till they both tuckered out.

And as they walked home,

Dotty thought of his day,

and all he had learned,

while he came here to play.

He said to his friend,

"I have learnt something new"

"If you give things a go,

you can learn something too".

The End

Story and Illustrations created by: Sophie Blokker

Flippy & Dotty Go To The Pond - First edition
National Library of New Zealand - ISBN: 978-0-473-67264-5

Published by Sophie Blokker - Artist www.sophieblokker.co.nz

www.ingramcontent.com/pod-product-compliance
Lightning Source LLC
Chambersburg PA
CBHW042112040426
42448CB00002B/238